For Emily – Lucy Fleming

Bloomsbury Publishing, London, Oxford, New York, New Delhi and Sydney

First published in Great Britain in 2017 by Bloomsbury Publishing Plc
50 Bedford Square, London WC1B 3DP

www.bloomsbury.com

BLOOMSBURY is a registered trademark of Bloomsbury Publishing Plc

Text by Teresa Heapy
Illustrations by Lucy Fleming
Text and illustrations copyright © Bloomsbury Publishing Plc 2017

The moral rights of the author and illustrator have been asserted

A CIP catalogue record of this book is available from the British Library

ISBN 978 1 4088 9001 1

All papers used by Bloomsbury Publishing are natural, recyclable products made
from wood grown in well managed forests. The manufacturing processes
conform to the environmental regulations of the country of origin

Printed in China by Leo Paper Products, Heshan, Guangdong

1 3 5 7 9 10 8 6 4 2

Princess Snowbelle
and the Snowstorm

Libby Frost

BLOOMSBURY

LONDON OXFORD NEW YORK NEW DELHI SYDNEY

Snowbelle, Princess of Frostovia,
stood in her turret window looking out
at the Opaline Mountains.

"Sparks, I'm so excited!"
she exclaimed to her white cat.
"But I'm a little bit scared, too"
she whispered.

"I've got to sing the Opening Song tonight at the Snow Ball
and I've never performed in front of the whole kingdom before!

Maybe I'll go and talk to Mum and Dad," said Snowbelle,
and Sparks meowed in agreement.

Princess Snowbelle ran from her bedroom
to the grand ballroom in the Opaline Palace.

The decorations weren't in place just yet
but the ballroom already shimmered and glowed,
and beautiful music was playing as her father and mother danced.

"Come and join us!" they called.
Snowbelle held her parents' hands,
and together they twirled around the room.

"Are you **nervous** about singing tonight?" said her mother.

"A little," admitted Snowbelle. "What if I make a mistake?"

"Don't forget you'll have your friend Sparkleshine with you," said her father.

"**Friendship** can help you get through **anything**."

Instantly, Snowbelle felt better.

"I'll do one more practice – and then I'll be ready!"

She kissed her parents and ran back to her room.

"All I need now is . . .
Sparkleshine!"

Snowbelle's friend, Sparkleshine,
was going to play the piano to accompany her.
"I hope she arrives soon!" said Snowbelle.
"She must be on her way,
through the forest . . ."

But then Snowbelle looked out of the turret window . . .

. . . and saw a huge snowstorm.
Suddenly snow was falling thickly
and it was almost impossible
to see through the trees.

"Oh no! Sparkleshine will
get lost and be alone!"
said Snowbelle.
"I must go and help her."

There was no time to lose. Snowbelle put on her warmest cloak
and rushed to the stables to saddle up her horse, Icetail.

"Come on, Icetail, we're going to find Sparkleshine!"
Icetail whinnied and stomped happily – she loved the snow.

Together, they set off into the heart of the snowstorm.
"Sparkleshine!" called Snowbelle. "Where are you?"

But all around them the snow whirled
and the wind blew, until all they
could see was a world of white.

"Icetail," said Snowbelle sadly, "I think we're lost!"

Suddenly she had an idea.
"I know," she said.
"To find Sparkleshine . . .
I can use my charm bracelet –
the one Mum and Dad gave me
for my first birthday!"

She shook her arm gently, and her delicate silver snowflake charm tinkled.
"We need light, little charm," whispered Snowbelle. "Light, to help us see!"

All at once, a beautiful pink light burst from the snowflake charm. It lit up a path through the forest.

"Sparkleshine must be this way!" said Snowbelle. "Come on, Icetail!"

They galloped through
the brightly lit forest.
A **squirrel** bounced onto the
path and ran ahead of them.

Soon a **blackbird** joined . . .

. . . and a family of **rabbits**.
"Look!" said Snowbelle.
"The animals are showing us the way!"

Before long, they reached a **huge** tree in the centre of the forest.
A gust of wind blew and **suddenly** they saw Sparkleshine huddled up,
shivering at the bottom of the tree.

"Oh, Snowbelle!" said Sparkleshine. "Thank goodness you're here!
I got lost, and had to find shelter!"

"We got lost, too – but we had
a little help!" smiled Snowbelle.
"Now – let's get back to the palace.
We don't want to miss the Snow Ball!"

Together, the friends darted through the
snowy forest, guided by Snowbelle's light.

When they came to the castle,
Snowbelle turned to her new forest friends.
"Thank you for your help. If you go into the kitchen
I think Cook might find you something to eat!"

The girls raced up to Snowbelle's bedroom.
Two beautiful dresses were hanging up ready for them.
Sparkleshine's was the colour of a pink sunset
and had a wide satin bow.
Snowbelle's was lilac and decorated
with patterns of twinkling stars.

"Oh!" said Sparkleshine. "I'm so very excited!"
"Me too," said Snowbelle, "and only a little bit nervous."

"Ready?" whispered Sparkleshine. "Ready!" smiled Snowbelle.
Holding hands, the two girls walked into the ballroom to wild applause.

"Welcome to the Snow Ball!" said Princess Snowbelle.
"And now, Sparkleshine and I are
going to perform the Opening Song!"

"You need never be afraid, on this you can depend.
Even in a whirling snowstorm . . ."

"You can always find a friend!"

"What a perfect Snow Ball!" said Snowbelle.
"Friendship and a little bit of magic really did get me through!"
She gently shook her charm bracelet to hear it tinkle.
"I can't wait for the next snowy day!"